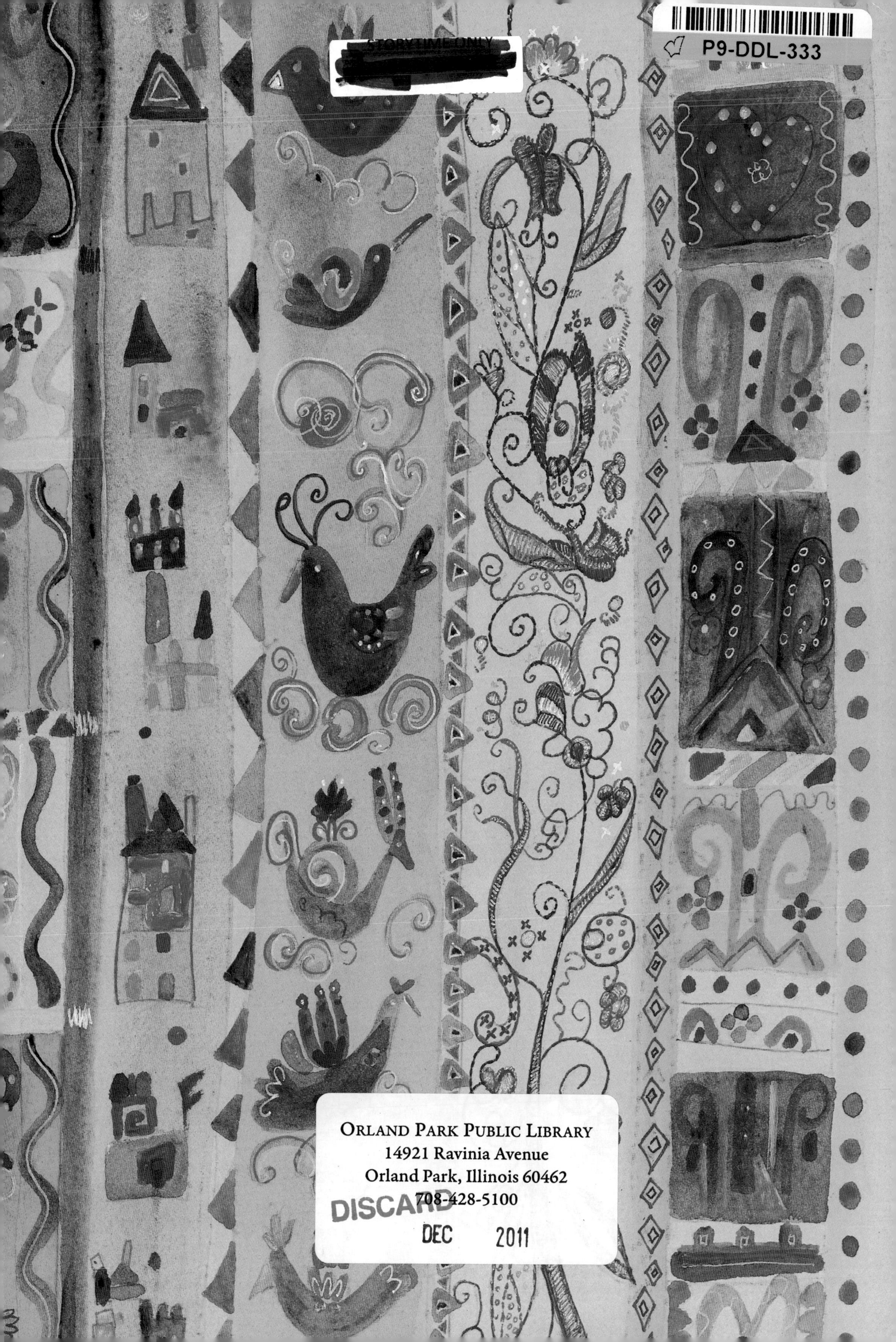

For Steve, Matthew and Tanda

About the story

The story of a hero who has to climb
a tree that reaches into the sky seems to have originated
in Hungary, with later versions recorded elsewhere in Eastern Europe.
This tale is based on a number of retellings including
"The Tree that Reached up to the Sky", (*Folktales of Hungary*,
edited by Linda Degh, published by
Routledge & Kegan Paul, 1965).

Climbing Rosa copyright © Frances Lincoln Limited 2006
Text and illustrations copyright © Shelley Fowles 2006

First published in Great Britain and in the USA in 2006 by Frances Lincoln Limited,
4 Torriano Mews, Torriano Avenue, London NW5 2RZ
www.franceslincoln.com

Distributed in the USA by Publishers Group West

British Library Cataloguing in Publication Data available on request

ISBN 1-84507-079-8

Set in Fontesque

Illustrated with pen and ink, and acrylics

Printed in China

3 5 7 9 8 6 4 2

Climbing Rosa

Shelley Fowles

FRANCES LINCOLN CHILDREN'S BOOKS

Long ago in a far-off kingdom there stood
an enormous tree. It was so tall that its highest branches
were hidden by clouds. No one had ever seen the top.

In the shadow of the giant tree stood a palace. There the king's
son Andras lounged around reading, day and night.
One evening, the king said crossly, "Enough! You're costing
me a fortune in candles. A wife would sort you out.

"I know – I'll hold a competition. The woman clever enough
to climb our tree and bring back some seeds can have
your hand in marriage. You shall be First Prize!"

Many tried...

...and many failed.

News of the contest spread
across the kingdom
and arrived just as a girl
called Rosa was climbing
up to bed.

Rosa could climb anything – which was just as well,
because her nasty stepmother and stepsister Irma
made her sleep out on the roof.

"You could win that contest, Rosa!"
said her stepmother. "You climb like a monkey!"
"She looks like a monkey too!" giggled Irma.
"The Prince would run a mile!"

"And you look like a poodle in a lampshade,"
thought Rosa. "It would be worth climbing
the tree just to get away from you."
"Follow her, Irma," hissed her mother.
"This could be your lucky day!"

When Rosa saw the Prince, she thought he was
gorgeous. Andras looked up from his book
and stared at her. "Maybe this contest isn't such
a bad idea," he thought.

Rosa started climbing. "This trunk is very smooth,"
she said, "but it's a doddle compared to the drainpipe
at home." She didn't realize that Irma was right
behind her, following her every move.

They climbed and they climbed. Suddenly, Rosa felt someone grab her – and there was Irma, hanging grimly on. "Don't let me fall!" cried Irma.

The ground
got further
and further
away.
"Don't push!"
whined Irma,
as Rosa
helped her up.
"Oh, stop
moaning!"
said Rosa.
"Who
asked you
to come
along,
anyway?"

Up and up they went.
Soon it was night.
"I'm scared!" moaned Irma.
"Don't worry," laughed Rosa.
"If there are any ghosts,
one look at you will
scare them away!"

Day broke.
Higher and higher they climbed,
towards the sun.

Suddenly Rosa spotted
an open pod full
of ripening seeds.
"I've found some seeds!"
she shouted.

Very carefully, Rosa picked the pod.

But Irma reached out and snatched it away.

"Thanks. I'm off!"

And she pulled Rosa right out of the tree.

"Now I'll never win the contest!" thought Rosa sadly

...as she fell down...

...and down...

...and down...

…and landed, CRASH! right on top of the Prince,
who was waiting eagerly below.
"Did you find any seeds?" he asked, picking himself up.

Rosa shook her head angrily. "That cheating,
over-dressed, half-witted…" she began furiously –

but as she spoke, clouds of seeds flew out
of her hair and landed at their feet.

Rosa married her delighted Prince
and the celebrations lasted for weeks.
As for Irma, she is still stuck up that tree.
"Maybe I will go and rescue her..."
Rosa said to Andras.
"But not yet!"